ISBN 0 86112 982 2
Published by Brimax Books Ltd, Newmarket, England 1994.
Printed in China

Frances Hodgson Burnett

THE
Secret Garden

Adapted by John Escott
Illustrated by Gavin Rowe

BRIMAX • NEWMARKET • ENGLAND

Introduction

Frances Hodgson Burnett's *The Secret Garden* has delighted generations of children since it was first published in 1911. It tells the story of Mary, a bad-tempered orphan, who is taken to Yorkshire, England to live in her uncle's huge house on the bleak Yorkshire moors.

While wandering around the grounds, Mary discovers a garden that is surrounded by a high stone wall. There does not at first appear to be a way in but Mary finds a key and then a door. Why, she wonders, is the garden locked up? What are those strange sounds that she hears at night? Mary is soon to discover the answers.

The beautiful illustrations along with the specially adapted text go together to make this a book that children will love to read.

Contents

The House on the Moor

MARY LENNOX was a thin, sickly-looking child with a sour face and a bad temper. She was born in India, where her father worked for the English Government. He was always busy with his work and saw little of his daughter, and Mary's mother was a beautiful woman who liked to go to parties, so Mary hardly ever saw her either.

She was looked after by an Indian nursemaid, called an Ayah, who did everything to please Mary so that the child would not cry or be a nuisance to her mother. So it was hardly surprising when Mary grew up into a spoilt little girl whom nobody liked.

One very hot morning, when Mary was nine years old, she awoke to find a new servant standing beside her.

"Why did you come?" she said to the strange woman. "Send my Ayah to me."

The frightened servant went away, but Mary's nursemaid did not come. Then Mary noticed some of the other servants were missing, too. It was all very strange. She began to feel something was very wrong, but nobody told her anything and all morning she played alone in the garden, becoming crosser and crosser.

It was later that day when Mary overheard her mother talking to a young man outside the house.

"Is it so very bad?" she heard her mother say.

"Very bad," the young man said. "You should have gone to the hills two weeks ago."

Slowly, as Mary listened to the two of them talking, it became clear what was happening. A bad disease was sweeping the country and many people

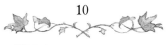

were dying. Some of their own servants were ill and others had run away. On hearing this, Mary became frightened and she ran to her room where she stayed for the rest of that day and all the next.

Nobody came to see her. Nobody even thought of her. She cried and slept, and slept and cried. Time passed and the house grew silent. She heard no footsteps, no sounds of voices, and *still* nobody came to see her.

The next time Mary awoke, the house was perfectly still. She lay quietly on her bed, and wondered what was happening outside. Had the sickness gone? Was everyone better? Surely someone would come soon.

And then she heard footsteps and the sound of two men talking.

After a while, the footsteps were outside her room, and suddenly the door opened.

"Barney!" the first man said. "There's a child here! A child alone. Who is she?"

"I am Mary Lennox," the little girl said crossly. "I fell asleep when everyone was ill and I've just woken up. Why does nobody come?"

"Poor thing," said the man. "There's nobody left to come."

And that was how Mary learned her father and mother had died.

Mary was quite alone. She had no family in India and there was no one left to look after her, so she was sent to England to live with her uncle, Mr Archibald Craven. Mary knew nothing about her mother's brother, but she was told he lived in a big house called Misselthwaite Manor in Yorkshire.

She made the long voyage to England and was met in London by a lady called Mrs Medlock, her uncle's housekeeper, a large woman with a red face and sharp black eyes. Mary did not like her. But then, Mary liked almost no one.

They travelled to Yorkshire by train, and Mary sat in the corner of the railway carriage looking plain and sulky in her black dress. She wondered why she always felt so alone. Other children seemed to belong to their parents, but even when her mother and father had been alive, Mary had never felt part of a family. She had always had clothes, and servants to look after her, but nobody had ever really loved her. She did not realise this was because she was such an unpleasant child.

"Do you know anything about your uncle?" Mrs Medlock asked her.

"No," said Mary.

"Did your father and mother not talk about him?"

"No," said Mary, frowning. Her father and mother had never talked to her about anything.

Mrs Medlock was silent for a while, then she said, "You're going to a strange place. It's six hundred years old – grand and gloomy, and standing on

the edge of the moors. There's nearly a hundred rooms in it but most of them are locked up. There's a big park around it, and gardens and trees …" She paused and took a breath. "But there's nothing else."

Mary pretended not to be interested.

"What do you think of it?" Mrs Medlock asked.

"Nothing," Mary answered. "I know nothing about such places."

Mrs Medlock laughed. "Eh!" she said. "You're like an old woman. Don't you care?"

"It doesn't matter whether I care or not," said Mary.

"You're right enough there," agreed Mrs Medlock. "Mr Craven isn't going to trouble himself about you, that's sure and certain. He never troubles himself about anyone. He's got a crooked back, and that made him a sour young man until he was married."

Mary's eyes turned towards her, in spite of trying not to be interested. She was suprised to hear Mr Craven was married.

"His wife was a sweet, pretty thing," Mrs Medlock went on, pleased that at last the child seemed to be interested in something. "He loved her more than anything in the world. Nobody thought she'd marry him, but she did. When she died – "

"Oh! Did she die?" said Mary, without meaning to. She was suddenly very sorry for Mr Craven.

"Yes, she died," answered Mrs Medlock. "And it made him quieter and stranger than ever. He cares about nobody, and won't see people. Most of the time he's away, and when he's at Misselthwaite Manor he shuts himself up in the west wing and only his servant sees him."

It sounded like something out of a book and did not make Mary feel very cheerful. A house with a hundred rooms, nearly all shut up, on the edge of a moor – whatever a moor was. And a man with a crooked back who shut himself away!

Mary stared out of the train window. Rain poured down in grey, slanting lines. She watched it until her eyes grew heavy, then she fell asleep.

It was dark when Mary awoke. She had been sleeping a long time, lulled by the splashing of the rain against the windows. Now the train had stopped and Mrs Medlock was shaking her.

"Wake up!" said Mrs Medlock. "We're at Thwaite station and we've a long drive ahead of us."

The station was a small one, and nobody but themselves seemed to be getting out of the train. Outside, a horse-drawn carriage was waiting for them and Mary was helped into it by a man wearing a long waterproof coat. The coat was shining and dripping with rain, as everything was.

She sat in the comfortable carriage and peered out into the darkness. Now

and then she caught a glimpse of whitewashed cottages or a church, but little else. Then they were on a high road and she saw hedges and trees, then nothing but darkness on either side.

"We're on the moor now," Mrs Medlock told her.

"What is a moor?" asked Mary.

"It's miles and miles of wild land," explained Mrs Medlock. "Nothing grows on it but heather and gorse, and nothing lives on it but wild ponies and sheep."

"It makes a noise like the sea," said Mary.

"That's the wind blowing through the bushes," Mrs Medlock said. "It's a wild, dreary place, I think. Though there's plenty that like it, especially in the Spring."

"I don't like it," Mary said to herself. "I don't like it."

After a while the carriage passed through some gates, then travelled along an avenue of tall trees. It stopped in front of a long, low house which was built around a courtyard. At first, Mary thought there were no lights in any of the windows, but then she saw a dull glow coming from an upstairs corner room.

A huge oak door was opened by a servant and Mary was taken into an enormous hall.

"You are to take her to her room," the servant told Mrs Medlock. "He doesn't want to see her. He's going to London in the morning."

Then Mary was led up a broad staircase and down a long corridor and up some steps and along another corridor and *another*, until a door opened in a wall. She found herself in a room with a fire in it and supper on a table.

"Well, here you are!" Mrs Medlock said. "This room and the next are where you will live – and you must stay in them. Don't forget it."

And so Mary Lennox began her life at Misselthwaite Manor, and she had never felt so cross and lonely.

Martha

WHEN MARY opened her eyes in the morning, a young housemaid was lighting the fire. Mary watched her for a few moments, then looked out of the window. She could see a large stretch of land, climbing into the distance and looking like an endless purple sea.

"What is that?" she asked the housemaid.

The girl's name was Martha and she smiled in a kindly way. "That's the moor," she said in her friendly Yorkshire voice. "Do you like it?"

"No," answered Mary. "I hate it."

"That's because you're not used to it," said Martha. "It's lovely in the Spring when the gorse and heather are in flower. The air smells of honey and the sky is blue and the birds sing. Eh! I wouldn't live away from the moor for anything!"

Mary was puzzled. She was not used to friendly servants. In India she had never said 'please' or 'thank you' and had once slapped her nursemaid when she was angry. Mary wondered what this girl would do if she slapped her. Slap her back, probably!

"Are you going to be my servant?" Mary asked.

"I'll help you a bit," said Martha, "but you won't need much help."

"Who is going to dress me?" demanded Mary.

Martha looked astonished. "Can't you dress yourself?"

"No," said Mary indignantly. "I've never done it in my life. My Ayah dressed me, of course."

"Well, it's time you learned!" Martha told her.

Mary was angry and confused. She suddenly felt so horribly lonely and far

away from the world she understood that she threw herself down on to her pillows and burst into tears.

Martha was a little frightened and felt quite sorry for her. She went over to the bed. "Eh! You mustn't cry like that!" she said kindly. "Get up now and I'll help you dress."

The clothes Martha took from the wardrobe were not those which Mary had worn the night before.

"Those aren't mine," said Mary. "Mine are black." She looked at the white coat and dress. "Those are nicer than mine."

"Mr Craven told Mrs Medlock to get them in London," said Martha. "He doesn't like black clothes."

"I hate black things," said Mary.

Martha chatted about her family as she helped Mary dress. At first, Mary was not at all interested, but slowly she began to listen to the friendly Yorkshire voice.

"Eh! You should see 'em all," Martha said. "There's twelve of us and my father only gets sixteen shillings a week. My mother's hard put to feed 'em all. They play on the moor, and our Dickon – he's twelve years old – he's got a wild young pony he calls his own. Dickon's a kind lad and animals like him."

Mary had never had a pet, but she'd always wanted one. She began to get interested in this boy who could tame wild animals. It was the first time she had ever been interested in anyone but herself.

They went into the next room where Mary's breakfast was waiting on the table. But Mary's appetite was small and she turned up her nose at the first plate Martha put in front of her.

"I don't want it," she said.

"You don't want your porridge?" exclaimed Martha. "Eh! I can't stand to see good food go to waste. Why, if our children were at this table, they'd clean it bare in five minutes!"

"Why?" asked Mary.

"Why? Because they scarcely ever have enough to fill their stomachs. They're always as hungry as foxes."

"Why don't you take it to them?" suggested Mary.

"It's not mine," answered Martha. "And it's not my day for going home. I get my day out once a month, then I go home and clean the house for my mother to give her a rest."

Mary drank some tea and ate a little toast and some marmalade.

"Wrap up warm and go outside to play," said Martha. "That'll give you an appetite."

"Who will go with me?" asked Mary.

Martha stared. "You'll have to learn to play by yourself like other children who don't have brothers or sisters. Our Dickon plays for hours on the moor."

Mary put on warm clothes and went out into the garden.

MARTHA

"There are lots of flowers in the summer," Martha told her, "but there's not much growing now because it's winter." She seemed to hesitate a second before adding, "One of the gardens is locked up. No one has been in it for ten years."

"Why?" asked Mary.

"Mr Craven had it shut when his wife died. He won't let anyone go inside. It was her garden. He locked the door and dug a hole and buried the key."

After Martha had gone back indoors, Mary walked through a gate into a large garden with wide lawns and clipped hedges. As she walked, Mary thought about the other garden – the one that nobody had gone into for ten years. What did it look like? Did flowers grow there? And why had Mr Craven shut it up and buried the key? If he had loved his wife so much, why did he hate her garden? She wondered if she would see Mr Craven, but even if she did she knew she would not like him, nor he her.

'People never like me,' she thought, 'and I never like people.'

At the end of the path where Mary was walking, there seemed to be a long wall covered in ivy. There was a green door in the wall and Mary opened it and walked through. She found herself in another garden with walls all around it, and that seemed to be only one of several. They each led into one another.

An old man was working in one of the gardens. He had a surly old face and did not seem pleased to see her, but then she did not look pleased to see him.

"What is this place?" asked Mary.

"One o' the kitchen gardens," he answered.

"What is that?" asked Mary, pointing to another green door.

"Another of 'em," he said, crossly.

"Can I go in?" she said.

"If you like," he said, "but there's nothing to see."

Mary went into the other kitchen garden. There were lots of fruit trees and another high wall, but this wall seemed to have no door in it. Mary decided this could not be the end of the garden because she could see the tops of more trees above and beyond the wall. On one of these trees was a small bird with a red breast. Suddenly, it burst into song, almost as if it had caught sight of Mary and was calling her. The cheerful sound brought a smile to her face and she listened until the bird flew away.

Mary walked back to the other garden where the old man was digging. She watched him for a while but he took no notice of her.

"I've been into the next garden," she said, "and I saw the other garden, the one without a door. There were trees there, and I saw a bird with a red breast on one of them. He was singing."

To her surprise, a smile spread slowly across the old man's face. Mary saw

how much nicer he looked when he smiled. Then the man turned towards the trees in the next garden and gave a soft whistle. And a wonderful thing happened. The little bird flew over the wall and landed next to the gardener's foot.

"Here he is," chuckled the old man. "Where have you been, little friend? I've not seen you today."

The bird put his tiny head on one side and looked at the man. Then he hopped about and pecked the earth, looking for seeds and insects.

"Will he always come when you call him?" asked Mary.

"Aye, he will," said the old man. "He's my only friend."

"What is he?" asked Mary.

"Don't you know?" said the gardener. "He's a robin, and he's all alone, like me."

"I don't have any friends," said Mary, looking at the robin.

The old man looked at her. "We're a good bit alike, you and me. We're neither of us good looking, and we've got the same nasty tempers, I expect."

"What is your name?" said Mary.

"Ben Weatherstaff," the man told her.

Suddenly, the robin flew on to the branch of a tree next to Mary and began to sing at the top of his voice.

Ben Weatherstaff laughed. "He's taken a fancy to you. He wants to be your friend."

"Do you really want to be my friend?" Mary asked the little bird. She spoke in a soft and kindly way, quite unlike her usual manner. Ben Weatherstaff looked surprised.

"Now you sound like a real child and not a cross old woman," he said. "It was almost like Dickon when he talks to his wild animals on the moor."

"Do you know Dickon?" Mary asked.

"Everyone knows Dickon," said the old man.

Mary wanted to ask him more questions about Dickon, but just then the robin flew away.

"He's flown over the wall into the garden with no door!" she cried, watching him.

"He lives there," said old Ben.

"There must be a door somewhere," said Mary.

"There was ten years ago," said Ben, "but it's not to be found now. Now don't go poking your nose into places where it's not wanted." He sounded cross again. "Go away, I've work to do."

And he walked off without saying goodbye.

The Cry in the Corridor

AT FIRST, each day that passed was exactly like the others. Every morning when Mary awoke, Martha was lighting the fire and a meal was waiting in the next room. Then she would play in the gardens, for there was nothing to do in the house. She ran around to keep warm and the cold wind brought a red glow to her face.

She went to one place more than any other. It was where she had seen the robin. The ivy grew thick on the walls there and the whole area looked especially neglected. Mary was wondering about this one day when she heard the bright chirping of the robin. She looked up – and there he was on the top of the wall.

"Oh, is it you?" she said.

The bird answered with a twitter and a chirp, and hopped along the wall. Mary laughed. "I like you, I like you!" she said.

The robin flew into the air and perched on a tree the other side of the wall.

"It's the garden without a door," Mary said to herself. "The secret garden. He lives in there. How I wish I could see what it's like."

That evening, when she was sitting down with Martha after supper, she asked a question she'd been wanting to ask for a long time.

"Why does Mr Craven hate the garden with no door?" she said.

At first Martha did not answer, but then she said, "It was Mrs Craven's garden. She made it when she and Mr Craven were first married, and she loved it. They looked after it together and no gardeners were ever allowed in there. But there was one old tree with a branch shaped like a seat, and Mrs Craven used to sit on it. One day when she was sitting there the branch broke

THE SECRET GARDEN

and she fell to the ground. She was hurt so badly that the next day she died. That's why Mr Craven hates it. The doctors thought he would go out of his mind and die too. Now he won't let anyone talk about it, and no one's gone in since."

Mary asked no more questions. She looked at the fire and listened to the wind howling outside the house. She felt very sorry for Mr Craven. It was the first time she had ever felt really sorry for anyone but herself, but now she understood how unhappy the man must be.

As Mary listened to the wind, she heard another sound. It was like a child crying, far away. She looked at Martha.

"Do you hear someone crying?" she said.

Martha looked startled. "No! It's the wind."

Suddenly, the door of the room blew open with a crash. Mary and Martha jumped to their feet. Now the crying was louder than ever.

"There!" said Mary. "I told you so! Someone *is* crying."

Martha ran and shut the door. "It – it was one of the servant girls," she said. "She's had toothache all day."

But Mary did not believe her.

Next day it rained heavily and when Mary looked out of her window the moor was hidden by a grey mist. There would be no going out that day.

"What do you do in your cottage when it rains like this?" she asked Martha.

"Try to keep out of each other's way, mostly," answered Martha. "Eh! There does seem a lot of us then. Dickon goes out, he doesn't mind the rain. He once brought home a fox cub that he'd found half drowned. Another time, he brought home a crow and tamed it."

"If I had a fox cub, I could play with it," said Mary.

Martha thought for a moment. "Can you knit?" she asked.

"No," answered Mary.

"Can you sew?"

"No."

"Can you read?"

"Yes," said Mary, "but my books were left in India."

"There's thousands of books in Mr Craven's library," said Martha. "Perhaps Mrs Medlock will let you go in there."

But Mary wanted to find it by herself. She also wanted to explore the rest of the house. Were there really a hundred rooms? Perhaps she could count the number of doors. It would be something to do.

She walked through the corridors, staring at the pictures on the walls. It seemed as if there was no one but her in the huge, rambling building. After a while, she climbed some stairs to the second floor, and it was here that she began to open doors. There were bedrooms and sitting rooms; rooms with paintings and strange furniture and curious ornaments.

Mary lost her way two or three times. She went back down to her own floor, but even then she could not find her room.

"How quiet everything is," she said to herself.

But then the silence was broken by a thin cry.

Mary's heart beat faster as she listened. 'It's nearer than it was last night,' she thought. 'And it *is* someone crying.'

Suddenly, a door opened at the end of the passage and out came Mrs Medlock. She was carrying a bunch of keys and looked angry when she saw Mary. "What are you doing here? Didn't I tell you to stay in your room?"

"I got lost," Mary said, "and I heard someone crying."

"Nonsense," said Mrs Medlock, "you didn't hear anything of the sort." And she took Mary's arm and pushed her down the passage until they were in front of Mary's room. Mrs Medlock pushed her inside, then said, "Now stay in there, or you'll find yourself locked up." She went out and slammed the door.

Mary went across to the fire, white with anger. "There *was* someone crying," she said to herself. "There was, there was!"

The Key

TWO DAYS later, Mary woke up and looked out of her window.

"Look at the moor!" she cried.

Outside, from a deep blue sky, a brilliant sun shone down across the moor. It looked quite different.

"I said you would like it after a bit," said Martha. "Just wait until you see the golden gorse and the heather flowering in the Spring."

"I should like to see your cottage," said Mary.

"It's my day off today, and I'm going home," said Martha. "I'll ask my mother about it. She's sensible and hard-working, and can nearly always see a way to do things."

"I like your mother," said Mary, "although I've never even seen her. And I like Dickon, but I've never met him either."

"I wonder what he would think of you?" said Martha.

"He wouldn't like me," said Mary in her stiff, cold little way. "No one does."

Martha hesitated, then said, "How do you like yourself, Mary?"

Mary thought about this. "Not at all – really," she answered. "But I've never thought about it before."

After Martha had gone home to see her mother, Mary felt very lonely. She went out into the garden and ran round and round in the sunshine until she felt better.

Ben Weatherstaff was working in the kitchen garden.

"Spring's coming," he told Mary. "The earth is ready to grow things. You'll see little green shoots coming through the soil soon."

"What will they be?" asked Mary.

THE KEY

"Crocuses and snowdrops and daffydowndillys. Have you never seen 'em?"

"No," said Mary. "Everything is hot and wet and green after the rains in India, and I think things grow up in the night."

"These won't grow so fast," said Ben. "You'll have to wait for 'em."

Very soon, she heard the soft rustling of wings and the robin appeared at her feet.

"Do you think he remembers me?" Mary asked Ben.

"Remember you!" said Ben. "Of course he does."

"Are things ready to grow in that garden where he lives?" said Mary.

"What garden?" said Ben, grumpily.

"The one where the old rose trees are. Are all the flowers dead?"

"Ask him," said Ben, looking down at the robin. "He's the only one who's seen inside it for ten years."

Ten years was a long time, Mary thought. She was born ten years ago. She walked away, thinking. She had begun to like the garden just as she had begun to like the robin and Dickon and Martha's mother. She was beginning to like Martha, too. There seemed to be such a lot of people to like – especially when you weren't used to liking!

Mary walked along by the wall where she had first seen the bird. And then the most wonderful thing happened, and it was all because of Ben Weatherstaff's robin.

The bird flew down on to the flowerbed near Mary, beside the wall.

"You do remember me!" she cried out happily. "You followed me."

Suddenly she saw something half buried in the earth, next to the robin. It was a rusty iron ring. Mary bent down and picked it up – and found it was more than a ring. It was an old key.

"Perhaps it's been buried for ten years," said Mary, her voice a whisper. "Perhaps … it's the key to the secret garden."

She looked at the key for a long time, turning it over and over in her fingers. Then she put it in her pocket and began to walk up and down beside the wall. It seemed so silly to have the key and yet not be able to find the door. But however hard she looked, she could not find it.

Mary went back to the house.

'I'll always keep the key with me,' she thought. 'Then if I ever *should* find the door, I'll have it ready.'

The next morning, Martha told Mary about her day at home.

"I told them all about you," said Martha. "Eh! And they were full of questions about India and the ship you travelled on to England. I couldn't tell them enough. Mother thinks you must be lonely, so she sent you a present."

It was a skipping rope, but Mary had never seen one before and Martha

had to explain how to use it. After that, Mary always took the rope when she went to play in the garden.

Later that morning, she was skipping near the place where she had found the key when the robin appeared. Mary laughed and skipped towards him. She could feel the heavy key in her pocket at each jump.

"You showed me where the key was yesterday," she said. "Will you show me the door today? I don't believe you know."

What happened next always seemed like a little bit of magic to Mary. The bird flew up on to the wall and began to sing. As he did so, a sudden gust of wind came from nowhere and blew some of the ivy away from the wall.

And Mary saw a round doorknob.

Her heart thumping, she put her hands under the ivy and began to pull it aside. There, under the thick curtain of leaves, was a door with a large, square lock. Mary's hand shook as she took the key from her pocket and fitted it into the lock.

It took two hands to turn it. She looked quickly around to make sure no one was coming, then took a deep breath and pushed the door. It opened slowly … slowly …

Mary slipped through, shutting the door behind her. Excitement rose up inside her and she could hardly breathe.

She was standing *inside* the secret garden!

Inside the Secret Garden

IT WAS a strange and mysterious place. The high walls that shut it in were covered in the thick stems of leafless rose trees. There were more trees growing up out of the winter-brown grass, and climbing roses had twisted around them and hung down like swaying curtains over the ground.

Mary did not know whether they were alive or dead. "How still everything is," she said. Even the robin on his tree was not making a sound. "And I'm the first person to speak in here for ten whole years."

She moved away from the door and walked under the arches of climbing roses. Were they all quite dead? Was it all a dead garden? Mary wished it wasn't.

The robin came down from the trees and hopped about or flew ahead of her between the bushes. It was as though he was showing Mary around the walled garden. Everything was overgrown, a tangle of weeds and brambles, but suddenly Mary saw some green shoots pushing up through the ground. She remembered what Ben had said and knelt down to look at them.

"Crocuses or snowdrops or daffydowndillys," she whispered to herself.

So the garden wasn't quite dead. Mary was pleased.

She knew nothing about gardening but the grass seemed to be growing too closely around the little green shoots, so she pulled some of it up to give the flowers more room to breathe.

"That's better," she said.

She went from place to place, digging and weeding with her fingers. It was hot work and soon Mary had taken off her coat and hat. By dinner-time, she had been working for almost three hours.

"I'll come back again this afternoon," she said happily.

Martha was surprised and pleased by how much dinner Mary ate. "So that's what skipping does for you!" laughed Martha.

She asked what Mary had done that morning, and Mary told her about the little green shoots in the ground, but she was careful not to mention which part of the garden she had been in.

"I wish I had a spade," said Mary.

"Whatever do you want a spade for?" said Martha, laughing.

"I – I'd like to make a little garden of my own," said Mary.

Martha's face lit up. "There now! That's just what my mother said you should do."

"How much would a little spade cost?" said Mary. "I have some money."

"Not much," said Martha. "I know! We'll write a letter and ask Dickon to buy you a spade and some seeds. He can bring them to you."

"Oh, yes, then I shall see him, too!" said Mary, pleased.

The sun shone down for nearly a week, and Mary went to the secret garden every day. Inside its beautiful old walls, she worked happily, and no one knew where she was.

Ben Weatherstaff never knew where she went.

"You're like the robin," he told her. "I never know when I'll see you or where you'll come from."

It was the end of the week when she saw Dickon. Mary was skipping through some trees on her way to the secret garden when she heard a low, whistling sound. She stopped and looked around. A boy was sitting under a tree playing a wooden pipe. He was about twelve years old, had a turned-up nose and his cheeks were as red as poppies. Above him, clinging to the trunk of the tree, was a squirrel; and quite near him were two rabbits, sitting up and listening.

When he saw Mary, he stopped playing and said, "Don't move or you'll frighten them." After a moment he stood up, but so slowly that he hardly seemed to move at all. At last the squirrel scampered up the tree and the two rabbits hopped away, but not as if they were in the least frightened.

"I'm Dickon," the boy said. "I've brought your garden tools. A spade, a rake, a fork and a hoe. Eh! And I've got some seeds."

"Will you show me the seeds?" said Mary.

They sat down and Dickon took a brown-paper package from his coat pocket. Inside were smaller packets, with pictures of flowers on them.

Dickon explained. "These are big red poppies, and they'll grow anywhere. And these white flowers smell the sweetest of all. They'll come up if you just whistle to 'em!" he joked. Then he turned his head quickly, his face lighting up. "Where's the robin that's calling us?"

THE SECRET GARDEN

"He's in that tree," said Mary. "He's Ben Weatherstaff's robin, but I think he knows me, too."

"Ay, he knows you," said Dickon. "And he likes you."

"Does he really?"

"He wouldn't come near if he didn't."

Dickon told Mary about the rest of the seeds, then he said, "Now then, where's this garden of yours?"

Mary's face went red, then became pale. She did not know what to say, and for a whole minute said nothing. Dickon watched her.

"Wouldn't they give you a bit of garden?" he asked.

Mary looked at him. "Can you keep a secret?"

"Aye," he said. "I can keep a secret."

She put out a hand and clutched his sleeve. "I've stolen a garden," she said quickly. "It isn't mine. It isn't anybody's. Nobody wants it or cares for it, only me."

"Where is it?" asked Dickon.

"I'll show you," said Mary.

She led him through the trees and along the path to the door in the wall. Then she pushed it open.

"Here it is," she said. "It's a secret garden."

Dickon looked around. "Eh!" he whispered. "It's a strange and pretty place. It's as if we stepped into someone's dream!"

6

"May I Have a Bit of Earth?"

FOR TWO or three minutes he stood looking round, then he began to walk as softly and carefully as Mary had walked the first time she had found herself inside the four walls.

"I never thought I'd see this place," he said, his voice a whisper.

"Did you know about it?" asked Mary.

She had spoken aloud and he signalled for her to be quiet. "We must speak softly," he whispered, "or someone will hear us and wonder what we're doing in here. Yes, I knew about this place. Martha told me how there was a garden nobody had been inside for ten years."

He stopped and looked at the tangle of rose trees around him.

"Are they all dead?" whispered Mary. "Can you tell?"

"Eh! No, not all of 'em. Although there's a lot of dead wood that needs to be cut out." He took a knife from his pocket and opened a blade.

Mary followed him from tree to tree, and he showed her the new shoots under the dead wood that he cut away. Next, he showed her how to use the spade and the hoe and the fork. Soon they were working together.

Suddenly, Dickon noticed some of the ground Mary had cleared earlier in the week. "Who did that?" he asked.

"I did," said Mary.

"Why, I thought you didn't know anything about gardening," he said.

"I don't," said Mary. "But the shoots were so little and seemed to want room to breathe."

"You were right," said Dickon. "They'll grow now. There's snowdrops and crocuses here. Oh, and here are some daffydowndillys!" He ran from one

clearing to another. "You've done a lot of work for a little girl."

"I'm growing stronger," said Mary. "I'm not tired when I dig now, and I love the smell of the earth."

"There's a lot to be done here," he said, looking round.

"Oh, please come again and help me!" said Mary.

"I'll come every day if you like, rain or shine," he said. "We'll have fun!" He began to walk about, looking at the trees and bushes and walls. "I don't want to make it look like a gardener's garden, all neat and tidy, do you? It's nicer when it's running a bit wild."

"Don't let's make it too tidy," said Mary. "It wouldn't seem like a secret garden if it was tidy."

They worked harder than ever, and Mary was sorry when it was time to go for her dinner. Dickon had his food with him, so he stayed behind in the garden.

"You – you'll never tell anyone about the garden, will you?" said Mary as she was about to leave.

He smiled. "Not me, Mary. You're as safe as the birds here."

And she was sure she was.

Her dinner was waiting on the table.

"You're a bit late," said Martha.

"I've seen Dickon!" said Mary. "And he – he's beautiful!"

Martha laughed. "I knew he would come," she said.

Mary ate her dinner quickly and Martha waited for her to finish before giving her some news.

"Mr Craven is back, Mary," she said. "He wants to see you."

Mary's face went white. "Why? He didn't want to see me when I arrived."

"He's going away tomorrow," said Martha, "and he wants to see you before he goes. He'll be away a long time, travelling in different countries. He won't be back until the autumn or winter."

Mary was glad he would be away so long. It would give her time to see the secret garden come alive. Then, if he took it away from her, it would not be so bad.

Mrs Medlock came to take her to see Mr Craven. She made Mary put on her best dress and brush her hair before they walked through the silent corridors of the big house. She was taken to a part she had not been to before. She was very nervous. At last, Mrs Medlock knocked on a door.

Mr Craven was sitting in an arm-chair by the fire.

"This is Mary, sir," Mrs Medlock said, then went out and closed the door behind her.

Mary waited, twisting her thin hands together. He was not so much a hunchback as a man with high, crooked shoulders, she saw. And his face would have been better looking if it had not been so miserable.

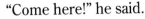

THE SECRET GARDEN

"Come here!" he said.

Mary went across. He looked anxious, as if he didn't know what to do with her. "Are you well?" he asked.

"Yes," said Mary.

"Do they take good care of you?"

"Yes."

"You are very thin."

"I'm getting fatter," she told him.

"I forgot about you," he admitted. "I was going to send you a nursemaid or a governess, but I forgot."

"I'm too old for a nursemaid," said Mary. "And please don't send me a governess, yet."

"What do you do?" he asked.

"I play out of doors. I skip and run. I don't do any harm."

"Don't look so frightened," he said. "You may do what you like. Is there anything you want?"

"May I have a bit of earth, to plant things and watch them grow?" asked Mary.

He gazed at her for a moment, then stood up and walked slowly across the room. "A bit of earth," he said softly. It was as though he was remembering something. "Do you care about gardens so much?"

"I didn't know about them in India," said Mary. "It's different here."

"You remind me of someone else who loved gardens," he said quietly. Then he turned and looked at her. "You can have as much earth as you want. Take it, and make it come alive. Now go, please, I'm tired, and tomorrow I'm going away. I'll be gone all summer."

Mary went back to her room and found Martha waiting.

"I can have my garden!" Mary told her. "Mr Craven is really a nice man, but he looks so sad."

Then she ran outside to look for Dickon. But when she went through the door of the secret garden, she couldn't see him anywhere.

"He's gone," she said, disappointed.

There was a piece of paper stuck on to the branch of a tree. A message had been written on it in big letters. It said:

"I WILL COME BACK."

Colin

IT RAINED heavily that night. Mary listened to it pouring down. The wind was making a moaning noise around the house and it kept her awake. She was twisting and turning in her bed when the noise changed.

"It's not the wind now," she whispered to herself, "it's that crying I heard before."

The door of her room was partly open and the thin, fretful sound came down the corridor. There was a candle beside her bed and Mary pushed back the bedclothes and picked it up. She took it to the doorway and looked along the dark corridor.

"I'm going to find out what that noise is," she said.

As Mary walked through the house, the noise came nearer and nearer. At last she stopped outside the room where she had seen Mrs Medlock that morning Mary had got herself lost. A glimmer of light came from beneath the door and the clear sound of somebody crying came from inside.

Mary opened the door.

It was a big room with a fire glowing faintly in the fireplace and a night-light burning beside a huge four-poster bed. A boy was lying on the bed, and he was crying pitifully. He had a pale face with eyes that seemed too big for it, and his hair was thick and dark.

Mary was standing in the doorway, the candle in her hand. The boy saw the light and stopped crying. He looked up.

"Who are you?" he said in a frightened whisper. "Are you a ghost?"

"No, I'm not," said Mary walking across the room. "Are you?"

"No," he replied. "I'm Colin Craven."

"I'm Mary Lennox," said Mary. "Mr Craven is my uncle."

"He's my father," said the boy.

"Your father!" said Mary. "Nobody told me he had a son."

"Come here," the boy said, and put out a hand to touch her arm. "You are real, aren't you? I thought you might be a dream."

"Did no one tell you I had come to live here?" said Mary.

"No," he answered. "They knew I wouldn't want you to see me. I don't want people to see me or talk about me."

"Why?" said Mary.

"Because I'm always ill. If I live, I shall be a hunchback. But I shan't live."

"Oh, what a strange house this is!" said Mary. "Everything is a secret. Rooms are locked up, gardens are locked up. Have *you* been locked up?"

"No," said the boy. "I stay here because I don't want to be moved."

"Does your father come and see you?" asked Mary.

"Sometimes," he said. "But he doesn't want to see me. My mother died when I was born and he remembers that whenever he looks at me. He almost hates me."

"He hates the garden because she died," said Mary.

"What garden?" asked the boy.

"Oh – just a garden she used to like."

"How old are you?"

"I'm ten," said Mary. "And so are you."

"How do you know?" he said.

"Because when you were born the garden door was locked and the key buried. And it's been locked for ten years."

Colin half sat up, leaning on his elbows. "What garden door? Who locked it? Where was the key buried?"

"Mr Craven locked it," said Mary. "No one knew where he buried the key."

"Have you asked the gardeners?" said Colin.

"They won't talk about it," she said.

"I could make them talk," said Colin. "They have to do as I say. If I live, Misselthwaite Manor will be mine one day. They all know that."

"Do you want to live?" asked Mary.

"No," he answered crossly. "But I don't want to die, either. I lie here and think about it until I cry."

"I've heard you crying," said Mary.

"Don't talk about that," he said. "Tell me about that garden. Do you want to see it?"

"Er … yes," said Mary.

"I do, too," he said excitedly. "I want the key dug up and the door unlocked. I want to go there in my chair. I'm going to make them open the door."

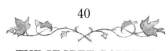

"Oh, don't do that!" pleaded Mary.

"Why?" said Colin. "You said you wanted to see it."

"If you make them open the door, it won't be a secret, don't you see? If – if there was a door … and we could find it … we could slip through it together and shut it behind us. It would be our secret garden."

Colin dropped back on his pillow and looked thoughtful. "I've never had a secret before," he said.

"Perhaps we could find a boy to push your wheelchair, and then we could go alone and it would always be a secret garden," she said. "I'll tell you what I *think* it would be like …"

And Mary began to describe the tangle of climbing roses, the old trees and the ivy-covered walls. Colin lay quite still and listened.

"What a lot of things you know," he said at last. "It's almost as if you'd been inside the garden already."

Mary did not know what to say. In the end, she asked, "Would Mrs Medlock be angry if she found me here?"

"She would do as I say," said Colin. "And I would say I wanted you to come here and talk to me every day. But I shall keep you a secret, too. I'll only tell Martha, then Martha can tell you when I want you to come here."

"Martha knew about you all the time?" said Mary. Now she understood why Martha had looked so troubled when Mary had asked her about the crying.

"She often looks after me," Colin said. He looked tired.

"You must go back to sleep now," said Mary.

"I wish I could go to sleep before you leave," he said shyly.

"In India, my Ayah used to sing me a song to help me sleep," said Mary. "I'll sing it to you."

She sang in a soft, sweet voice until slowly … slowly … Colin's eyes closed and he went to sleep. Then Mary took her candle and crept away without making a sound.

8

"She Makes Me Feel Better!"

THE MOOR was hidden in a mist the next day, and the rain still poured down. Martha was busy that morning, but in the afternoon she came to sit with Mary.

"I've found out what the crying was," said Mary.

Martha looked afraid. "Oh, no!" she cried.

"I heard it in the night," Mary went on, "and I went to see where it came from. It was Colin. I found him."

"Eh! Miss Mary, you shouldn't have done that!" said Martha, half crying. "You'll get me into terrible trouble. I didn't tell you anything about him, but I shall lose my job. Then what'll Mother do?"

"You won't lose your job," said Mary. "He was glad I came, and we talked and talked. I told him about India and the gardens and the robin. Then I sang him to sleep."

Martha gasped with amazement. "I can't believe it! He never lets strangers even look at him."

"He let me look at him," said Mary.

"If Mrs Medlock finds out – " began Martha.

"He's not going to tell her," said Mary. "It's going to be a sort of secret at first. I think he likes me. What's the matter with him?"

"Nobody knows for sure," said Martha. "After his wife died, Mr Craven didn't want to see the boy. He said the child would be just another hunchback like himself."

"Colin didn't look like a hunchback."

"He isn't yet," said Martha, "but they've always been afraid his back was

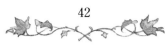

weak and they've never let him walk. A famous doctor once came to see him. He said Colin would get better if less fuss was made about his back and if he didn't get his own way so often. But nobody took any notice of this."

"I think Colin's a very spoiled boy," said Mary.

"He is," agreed Martha.

"Perhaps he'd be better if he went out into the garden," said Mary. "It did me good to go out into the fresh air and watch things growing."

"They took him out once," said Martha. "He began to sneeze and said he'd caught a cold. Then a new gardener looked curiously at him, and Colin got angry and said the gardener was staring because he knew Colin was going to be a hunchback. He cried so much he was ill all night."

"If he gets angry with me," said Mary, "I won't go and see him again."

Later that afternoon, Martha came to tell Mary that Colin wanted to see her.

"It's like magic," said Martha. "He's out of bed and sitting on his sofa with his picture books! And he's told his nurse to stay away until six o'clock."

Martha waited outside when Mary went into Colin's room. It was a very beautiful room, Mary saw now that it was daylight. There was a warm fire, and pictures on the walls, and colourful rugs on the floor. Colin was wearing a velvet dressing gown.

"I've been thinking about you all morning," he said.

"Poor Martha is afraid of losing her job," said Mary. "She's afraid Mrs Medlock will think she told me about you."

"Tell Martha to come here," said Colin, frowning.

Mary fetched her.

"Have you to do as I say, or not?" Colin said to Martha.

"Yes, sir," said Martha, nervously.

"Has Medlock to do as I say?" asked Colin.

"Everybody has, sir," said Martha.

"So, if I tell you to bring Mary to me," said Colin, "Medlock cannot send you away, can she? In fact, I'll send *her* away if she says a word about such a thing."

"Thank you, sir," said Martha.

After Martha had gone, Mary told Colin about Dickon, but she didn't mention the secret garden.

"He's not like anyone else in the world," said Mary. "He can charm foxes and squirrels and birds. He plays a tune on a pipe and they come to listen. He says it's because he knows their ways."

"Does he like the moor?" said Colin. "It's such a big dreary place."

"It's the most beautiful place!" said Mary. "I only drove over it in the dark, but when Dickon talks about it, you feel as if you're standing in the heather with the sun shining on you, and the birds and butterflies around you."

"You never see anything when you're ill," grumbled Colin.

"You can't if you stay in here," said Mary.

"I can't go on to the moor," he said.

"You might, one day," said Mary.

"How could I? I'm going to die," he said.

"How do you know?" said Mary, crossly. She didn't like the way he talked about dying, almost as if he was pleased about it.

"Everyone whispers about it when they think I don't notice," said Colin. "They want me to die. Dr Craven, my father's brother, wants me to die. My father will be glad, too."

"I don't believe that," said Mary.

"Don't you?" said Colin.

"No," said Mary. "What about that famous doctor who came to see you? Did he say you were going to die?"

"No," admitted Colin. "He said I might live if I made my mind up to do it."

"Dickon would cheer you up," said Mary. "He talks about living things, not dead things." She told him about Dickon's mother and the little cottage on the moor. She told him about the skipping rope and Ben Weatherstaff's robin. Soon they were laughing together and Colin had forgotten all about his weak back.

It was in the middle of all this that Dr Craven – Mr Craven's brother – and Mrs Medlock walked in. They both looked shocked at what they saw.

"What's this?" said Dr Craven. "What does it mean?"

"This is Mary Lennox," said Colin. "I asked her to come and talk to me. She must come whenever I send for her."

Dr Craven looked angrily at Mrs Medlock.

"I don't know how it happened, sir," she said quietly. "None of the servants would dare talk."

"Mary heard me crying and came and found me," said Colin, "and I'm glad she came."

Dr Craven did not look pleased. "There's been too much excitement," he told Colin. "Excitement isn't good for you, my boy."

"She makes me feel better," said Colin. He looked at Mrs Medlock. "Mary and I will have tea together. Bring her tea in with mine."

Dr Craven told Colin to remember he was ill and became tired easily.

"I don't want to remember it!" said Colin. "And Mary helps me forget it."

The doctor did not look happy when he and Mrs Medlock left the room.

9

The Quarrel

IN THE week that followed, the rain kept Mary away from the secret garden. Instead, each day she went to see Colin and they talked about India or Dickon or the cottage on the moor.

She wondered if he could be trusted to keep a secret. She was sure the gardens and fresh air would be good for him, but would he tell people about the secret garden if she took him there? Also, if he hated people looking at him, would he want to meet Dickon?

On the first sunny morning after the rain, Mary woke early. She ran to the window and looked out. The moor was blue like the sky, and the birds were singing. She opened the window and put her head out.

"It's warm!" she said. "I can't wait to get to the garden!"

She had learned to dress herself by this time, and quickly put on her clothes. Down the stairs she flew, and out into the sunshine.

Mary ran towards the secret garden, the sun pouring down on her face. 'Dickon will come this afternoon,' she thought.

The rain had helped the grass to grow greener and the little shoots to push themselves higher out of the ground. Things were sprouting and growing everywhere now.

Mary reached the door of the secret garden and went in. And there was Dickon, working hard, a bushy-tailed little animal watching him.

"Oh, Dickon!" said Mary. "How could you get here so early? The sun has only just got up!"

Dickon looked up and laughed. "Eh! I was up before the sun. How could I have stayed in bed? It's such a lovely morning." He rubbed the little animal's

head. "This is the little fox cub. It's name is Captain."

The fox cub did not look in the least nervous of Mary, and when Dickon began to walk around, it trotted behind him. They looked at a clump of purple and orange crocuses, saw the buds on rose branches that had looked dead only a few weeks earlier.

Suddenly, a flash of red flew across the wall and darted through the trees. It was the robin, and he settled in a big tree in the corner.

"He's found a mate and is building a nest in that tree," said Dickon. "We must be careful not to frighten him away. Try not to watch him."

"Then I'll talk about something else," said Mary. "Do you know about Colin?"

He turned his head to look at her. "What do *you* know about him?"

"I've seen him. I've talked to him every day this week. He says I make him forget about being ill and dying."

Dickon smiled. "I'm glad you've found out about him. I didn't like keeping him a secret from you."

"How did you know about Colin?" asked Mary.

"Mrs Medlock stops at our cottage sometimes and talks to Mother," said Dickon. "She knows she can trust us to say nothing about the boy. But we know he's a hunchback and that Mr Craven can't bear to see him."

"He isn't a hunchback," said Mary, "but he's afraid he's going to be one. He just lies there thinking about it."

"He'd stop thinking about it if he could see the rose bushes and the plants growing out here," said Dickon, rubbing the neck of the little fox cub and looking around the garden.

"I've thought that, too," said Mary. "I've wondered if we could bring him out in his wheelchair. I'm sure he'd get better in the fresh air."

And so it was decided. They would bring Colin out to the secret garden as soon as they could.

Mary went back to the house for her dinner, but as soon as she had finished, she wanted to get back to the garden.

"Tell Colin I can't come and see him yet," she said to Martha. "I'm busy in the garden."

Martha looked worried. "He may be angry," she said.

"I can't help that," said Mary. "Dickon will be waiting for me."

And she and Dickon worked in the garden all afternoon, busier than ever. The robin and his mate were also keeping busy, flying backwards and forwards like little streaks of red lightning as they built their nest.

It was evening before Mary got back to the house. She wanted to tell Colin about Dickon's fox cub and the robin, but when she saw Martha she knew something was wrong.

THE SECRET GARDEN

"Eh!" said Martha, "Colin had the most terrible tantrum because you didn't go to see him. He's been angry all afternoon."

Mary made a face. She liked the garden and she saw no reason why a bad-tempered boy should stop her from going there.

He was not on his sofa when she went into his room. He was lying flat on his back on the bed.

"Why didn't you get up today?" asked Mary.

"I did get up this morning when I thought you were coming," he answered. "Why didn't you come?"

"I was working in the garden with Dickon," said Mary.

Colin scowled. "I won't let that boy come here if you go and stay with him instead of coming to talk to me."

Mary became very angry. "If you send Dickon away, I'll never come here again," she said.

"You'll have to if I want you," said Colin.

"I won't!" shouted Mary.

"I'll make you," said Colin. "I'll make them drag you in."

"They can't make me talk when they get me here," snapped Mary. "I'll sit here and say nothing."

They scowled at one another in silence.

Then Colin said, "You're a selfish thing!"

"I'm not as selfish as you!" said Mary. "You're the most selfish boy I ever saw!"

Colin turned away and shut his eyes and a big tear was squeezed out and ran down his cheek. "I – I'm ill and I'm going to die," he said.

"You're not," said Mary. "You just say that to make people sorry for you and to make them do as you tell them."

"Get out of my room!" shouted Colin, and he threw his pillow at her.

"I'm going, and I won't come back," said Mary. "I was going to tell you about Dickon and his fox cub, but I won't now."

She marched out of the room and shut the door behind her.

Martha was waiting in Mary's room. Her worried look had been replaced by one of curiosity. There was a wooden box on the table with some packages inside.

"Mr Craven sent it," Martha told Mary.

Mary opened one of the packages and found some books inside. Beautiful books with pictures in them, and two that were all about gardening. In another package were some games, and in another some writing paper and a gold pen and ink stand.

As Mary looked at her presents, her anger faded away. It was kind of Mr Craven to give her these things.

THE SECRET GARDEN

"I'll use my pen and paper to write him a letter, thanking him," she told Martha.

If she hadn't just argued with Colin she would have run and showed him her presents right then. He would have liked to see them, she was sure. It would have made him feel better. There was so little to cheer him up.

She began to feel sorry for him again. 'I said I would never go back,' she thought, 'but perhaps I'll go back and see him tomorrow.'

10

A Tantrum in the Night

IT SEEMED to be the middle of the night when Mary woke up.

"What's that noise?" she said to herself.

Doors were opening and closing, feet were hurrying along the corridors – and someone was crying and screaming at the same time.

"It's Colin," she said. "He's having a bad tantrum."

The bedroom door opened and Martha came in. "Oh, Miss Mary!" she said. "Nobody can do anything with him, and we're afraid he'll do himself some harm. Can you come? He might listen to you."

"All right," said Mary, "but remember he turned me out of his room this morning."

She followed Martha to Colin's room. The boy was lying on his face, beating the pillow as he screamed and cried.

"Stop it at once!" shouted Mary. "If you scream another scream, I'll scream too! And I can scream louder than you! I'll frighten you."

He turned round, startled by the furious little voice. His face was red and swollen, and he was gasping and choking. "I – I can't stop," he sobbed.

"You can!" Mary shouted.

"I felt the lump on my back," he sobbed. "I shall have a hunch on my back and I'll die."

"No you won't," said Mary. "Turn over and let me look at your back."

It was a poor, thin back. Mary looked up and down it.

"There's not a single lump there," she said at last. "If you ever say there is again, I shall laugh."

Colin's sobbing died away. "Do – do you think I'll live to grow up?" he said.

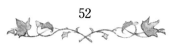

"You will if you don't have tantrums, and if you go out into the fresh air," said Mary.

"Will you and Dickon push my chair?" said Colin. "I do so want to see Dickon and the fox cub."

"Yes," said Mary, "but now you must go to sleep. I'll sing to you, if you like."

"Oh, yes," said Colin. Then, when Martha had gone out of the room, he whispered: "Have you found out any more about the secret garden?"

"Ye-es," answered Mary. "I think so. If you go to sleep, I'll tell you tomorrow." And she began to sing.

Colin closed his eyes, and very soon he was fast asleep.

Mary slept late the next morning, but as soon as she was up she went to the secret garden to find Dickon. He was there with his little fox cub and two tame squirrels, and he listened carefully as she told him about Colin's tantrum in the night.

When she had finished speaking, Dickon looked around him at the garden. "Just listen to those birds," he said. "And look how green and alive everything is. Eh! We must get that little lad out here. He'll feel better in no time."

Mary went back to the house to see Colin. To begin with, she talked about Dickon and his animals and Colin listened quietly.

"I wish I was friends with things," he said at last. "And I'm sorry I said I'd send Dickon away. I hated him because you liked him, but now I want to see him."

"I'm glad you said that," answered Mary, "because – " She stopped and looked at him. "Can you keep a secret? Can I trust you for *sure*?"

"Yes!" said Colin.

"Well, Dickon will come and see you tomorrow morning, and he'll bring some of his animals with him."

"Oh!" Colin cried with delight.

"But that's not all," said Mary. "There's a door in the garden, and I've found the key."

Colin's eyes opened wide. "Will I see it?" he asked, his voice a half-whisper. "Will I see inside the secret garden?"

"Of course you will." Mary hesitated, then she told him the truth, the words coming out in a rush. "I've seen inside the garden. I found the key weeks ago, but I was afraid to tell you in case I couldn't trust you for *sure*."

Garden Magic

DR CRAVEN came to see Colin later that morning.

"How is he?" he asked Mrs Medlock as they went up to Colin's room.

"You'll hardly believe your eyes when you see him," said Mrs Medlock.

They found Colin in his dressing gown, sitting on the sofa in his room. He and Mary were talking and laughing. Dr Craven looked surprised.

"I'm sorry to hear you were ill last night, my boy," said the doctor.

"I'm much better now," said Colin. "I'm going out in my chair in a day or two, if it's fine."

Dr Craven looked alarmed, but there was nothing he could do. "Who will push your chair?" he said.

"Dickon can do it," Mary said quickly. "He's very strong."

Dr Craven knew Dickon, and that made him feel a little better about it. "Very well," he said.

That night, Colin slept without waking once, and when he opened his eyes he smiled. For the first time, he was comfortable and happy and not worrying about his back.

Mary arrived soon after. "I've seen Dickon," she said. "He's bringing the fox, a tame crow and a new-born lamb that's lost its mother."

They heard him coming along the corridor, then Dickon came in smiling his nicest smile. The new-born lamb was in his arms and the little red fox trotted by his side. The tame crow was on his shoulder.

Colin stared in wonder and delight as Dickon came across and put the little lamb on Colin's lap. It buried its nose in Colin's dressing gown.

"It wants feeding," said Dickon, and he took a feeding bottle from his

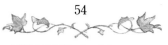

THE SECRET GARDEN

pocket. He knelt down beside Colin and put the feeding bottle into the lamb's mouth. "I knew you'd like to see it feed."

Colin watched with amazement as the little creature took its food and then fell asleep on his lap. Afterwards, Dickon talked about all his animal friends and Mary and Colin listened to him, spellbound.

Then Mary showed Colin some of the flowers in her picture books. "These are snapdragons," she said, pointing to a picture. "There's a big clump of them in the secret garden."

"And I'm going to see them!" said Colin. "I'm going to see them all!"

However, they had to wait a week before Colin could be taken into the garden. At first the days were too windy, then Colin caught a cold.

Then came the day when Colin was put into his chair and taken outside. He turned his face up to the sky and breathed in the sweet-smelling air that the soft wind blew down from the moor.

"What's that lovely smell?" he wanted to know.

"It's the gorse on the moor," said Dickon.

"And listen to the sounds of the birds!" said Colin, laughing.

Dickon pushed him along the paths, beside the ivy-covered walls.

"This is the garden where Ben Weatherstaff works," Mary told him. "And now we're coming to the place where I found the key, thanks to my friend the robin."

Dickon pushed the chair over to the wall and Mary lifted aside the curtain of ivy. "And this is the door!" she said. "Push Colin inside quickly, Dickon."

Colin closed his eyes and did not open them until he was inside the secret garden. Then he looked … and gasped with delight. He looked round and round, just as Mary and Dickon had done, the warm sun on his face and the sweet smells of the flowers around him.

"I shall get well!" he cried out. "And I shall live for ever and ever!"

Colin watched Mary and Dickon working. They brought him things to look at – buds that were opening, the feather of a woodpecker – and he sat in his chair under the plum tree and thought how wonderful everything was.

"I wonder if we shall see the robin?" he asked a little later when Dickon was pushing the wheelchair around the garden.

Then he noticed an old, old tree covered in roses. The tree itself was quite dead, but the roses had clambered all over it.

"One of the branches has been broken off," said Colin.

Dickon and Mary looked at one another.

"Aye," said Dickon. "It happened many years ago."

Suddenly, the robin flew over the wall and Colin forgot about the tree with

the broken branch. "There he is!" cried Colin, smiling broadly.

Afterwards, Mary always thought the sudden appearance of the robin was like a bit of magic. For both she and Dickon had been afraid Colin might ask them about the tree with the broken branch. The tree where the accident with his mother had happened so long ago. But the robin had saved them.

"I don't want the afternoon to end," said Colin. "But I'll come back tomorrow, and the day after, and the day after that. I've seen the Spring and I'm going to see the Summer. I'm going to see everything grow here. I'm going to grow here myself!"

"So you will," said Dickon. "Eh! We'll soon have you walking and digging like us."

"Walking! Digging!" Colin's face was filled with excitement.

"For sure you will," said Dickon. "You've got legs, haven't you?"

"But they're so weak and thin," said Colin. "I'm afraid to try and stand on them."

"When you stop being afraid you'll be able to stand on them," said Dickon.

The sun was dropping lower in the sky. The afternoon was almost over and the garden was still and quiet now. Then, in the midst of this stillness, Colin looked up and saw a face above the wall.

"Who is that man?" he said, pointing to the top of the wall.

Mary and Dickon looked up to see Ben Weatherstaff's face staring down at them. He was standing on top of a ladder and looked very angry and was shaking his fist at Mary.

"You bad girl!" he said. "What are you doing in there?"

And then the old man saw Colin and his mouth fell open in surprise.

"Do you know who I am?" said Colin.

Ben Weatherstaff stared, unable to believe what he was seeing. "Aye, that I do," he said. "You have your mother's eyes. But aren't you a cripple?"

"No, I'm not!" said Colin, furiously. "Watch me!" He waved to Dickon. "Come here, Dickon."

And with Dickon holding his arm, Colin threw off the blanket covering his legs – and stood up!

"Look at me!" said Colin. "Am I a hunchback?"

"No, lad," said old Ben, tears coming to his eyes. "You'll make a man yet, God bless you."

"Now climb down your ladder and wait by the wall," said Colin. "Mary will bring you into the garden. I want to talk to you."

Whilst Mary went to fetch the old man, Colin said to Dickon, "I'm going to walk to that tree. I want to be standing by it when Weatherstaff comes in."

And he walked with Dickon holding on to his arm. When Ben Weatherstaff came into the garden, he was astonished to see Colin standing by the tree.

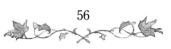

THE SECRET GARDEN

He looked around. "This was your mother's garden, and she loved it," he said.

"It's mine now," said Colin, "and I love it, too. You must promise to keep it a secret. Only Mary, Dickon, you and me must know."

Ben promised.

Dr Craven had been waiting some time when they returned to the house.

"You should not have stayed so long," he said to Colin.

"I'm not tired at all," said Colin. "Tomorrow I shall go out in the morning as well as the afternoon."

So Colin began to go to the garden every day, and it seemed that the garden began to work its magic on the boy. As the plants pushed up through the earth and burst into beautiful flowers, so Colin grew stronger and stronger.

One day, he announced: "I am going to walk round the garden."

And, with Dickon on one side of him, Mary on the other, and Ben Weatherstaff behind him, Colin walked slowly round the garden.

"The magic is making me strong!" said Colin. "I can feel it in me!"

"What will Dr Craven say?" said Mary.

"He won't say anything," answered Colin. "I'm not going to tell him. It's to be the biggest secret of all. No one at the house is to know anything about it until I've grown strong enough to walk and run like any other boy. I'll come here each day in my wheelchair and no-one will know. Then when my father comes back, I shall walk into his study and say, 'Here I am, just like any other boy. I'm quite well and I'm going to live to be a man.'"

"He'll think he's dreaming," said Mary.

Dickon's Mother

ONE OTHER person did learn about Colin and the secret garden. It was Dickon's mother, Mrs Sowerby. Dickon told her one evening after she had teased him about spending so much time at Misselthwaite Manor with 'Miss Mary'.

He told her the whole story and she listened in amazement. "My word!" she said when he had finished. "It was a good thing that little lass came to the Manor. It's been the making of her and the saving of Colin. What do the people at the house think? They must have noticed how much more cheerful the boy's become."

"They don't know what to make of it," said Dickon. "He looks so much better, his cheeks all red and healthy from the sun."

Every day when the weather was fine, Colin walked in the garden amongst the trees and flowers. Then Dickon showed him some simple exercises to strengthen his muscles, and soon Colin was helping with the weeding and digging.

He was always hungry now, but he didn't want the servants at the house to notice how much his appetite had improved, so he wasn't able to ask for extra food. Then Dickon had an idea. He told his mother about Colin's appetite and Mrs Sowerby began to send freshly baked currant buns and rich creamy milk for the children to share.

"Your mother is very kind, Dickon," said Colin.

Several days later, after it had rained for almost a week, the children and Ben Weatherstaff were working in the garden when Colin stopped and looked up. A woman was coming through the door. The sunlight shone through the trees and dappled her long blue cloak as she smiled at the three of them.

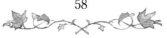

"Who is it?" Colin said, startled.

"It's Mother, that's who it is!" laughed Dickon. "I knew you wanted to see her, so I told her where to find the door to the garden."

Colin looked at her shyly. "I wanted to see you, even when I was ill," he said. "You and Dickon and the secret garden. And I'd never wanted to see anything or anybody before."

Her eyes became misty with tears. "Eh! Dear lad!" she said.

"Are you surprised I'm so well?" said Colin.

She put a hand on his shoulder and smiled. "Aye, that I am," she said. "But you're so like your mother you made my heart jump."

"Do you think my father will like me?" he asked.

"Aye, he will," she answered.

Ben Weatherstaff moved closer to her. "Look at the lad's legs," he said. "They were like drumsticks in stockings two months ago. Look at 'em now!"

Mrs Sowerby laughed. "They're going to be fine strong legs soon," she said. Then she turned to Mary. "And you've grown strong and healthy, too. Aye, and pretty!"

They took Mrs Sowerby round the garden, telling her the whole story of it and showing her every bush and tree which had come alive. She listened and seemed to understand in the way Dickon understood his animals, stooping over the flowers and talking about them as if they were children.

She had brought a basket of food with her and when the children became hungry, they sat under a tree and had a picnic. Mrs Sowerby watched happily as they joked and laughed together.

After a while, Colin looked at her and said, "Do you think my father will come home soon?"

"Aye, he must," said Mrs Sowerby.

"I think about him a lot now," said Colin. "I think about how I'll run into his room and surprise him."

"I'd like to see his face, lad," said Mrs Sowerby, "I would that!"

Another thing they talked about was a visit to Mrs Sowerby's cottage. They planned how they would drive over the moor and eat their lunch out of doors amongst the heather. How they would see all the twelve children and Dickon's garden, and how they would not come back until they were tired out.

At last, it was time for Mrs Sowerby to go home and for Colin to go back to the house. He looked at her kindly face and caught hold of her blue cloak.

"You were just what I wanted," he said. "I wish you were my mother as well as Dickon's!"

Mrs Sowerby's eyes became misty again and she drew him towards her. "Eh! Dear lad," she said. "Your father must come back to you soon – he must!"

Mr Craven Comes Home

AS TIME went on, Mary became a very different person to the spoilt, disagreeable little girl who had first come to Misselthwaite Manor. Her head was no longer full of sour and selfish thoughts. Instead, she was busy thinking about Dickon, the robin, moorland cottages crowded with children, and her beautiful secret garden.

Colin, too, had changed. When he had been shut up in his room, he had thought only about his fears and his illness and dying. He knew nothing of the sunshine or of Spring. He didn't know he could get well, or stand on his feet if he tried to do it. But when the magic of the garden began to work on him, he too became a different person.

As the secret garden came alive, so too did Mary and Colin.

Whilst all this was happening, Colin's father was wandering around the most beautiful parts of Europe, in countries like Norway and Switzerland. But his heart was filled with sadness, as it had been for ten long years. The blue lakes, the mountain sides covered with flowers – none of this brought him happiness, and his thoughts remained dark and restless.

It was one day when he was walking amongst the beautiful hills and valleys of Austria that something happened. He had walked a long way that day and had become very tired. Wearily, he dropped down beside a clear mountain stream and rested his head on a carpet of moss.

The valley was very still and silent. Just the sound of the running water as it bubbled and splashed over stones. As Mr Craven gazed into the clear water, he felt his mind and body grow quiet … as quiet as the valley itself. At first he thought he was going to sleep, but he did not. Instead, he watched the sunlit

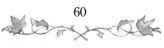

water, and his eyes began to see what was growing at its edge – a mass of blue forget-me-nots, so close to the stream that its leaves were wet and shiny.

He did not know how long he lay there watching the stream, but at last he got up and stood beside the water. He moved as if awakening from a dream – and for the first time in ten years he felt calm and at peace with himself.

That night he slept well and, in the morning, continued his travels. On to Italy, and the beautiful Lake of Como. The golden summer had changed into a deeper golden autumn. Mr Craven spent his days beside the crystal blue lake or walking in the soft green hills around.

Then one night he had a dream. A dream so real that he did not feel he was dreaming at all. He heard a voice calling. A sweet, clear voice.

"Archie! Archie!" it called.

"Lilias!" he answered. "Where are you?"

"In the garden!" said the voice of his wife. "In the garden!"

And then the dream ended.

When he awoke the next morning, there was a letter waiting for him. He opened it and began to read:

Dear Sir,

I am Susan Sowerby who spoke to you once on the moor. I hope you will not be angry because I have written but, please sir, I would come home if I was you. I think you would be glad if you did. Come as quickly as you can.

Your obedient servant,

Susan Sowerby

Mr Craven read the letter twice. He kept thinking about his dream.

"I'll go back to Misselthwaite," he said. "Yes, I'll go at once."

On the journey home, he found himself thinking of his son. For the past ten years he had only wished to forget about the boy, but now memories of him drifted into his mind. He had not meant to be a bad father but, after his wife died, Mr Craven had not felt like a father at all and had kept away from the sickly-looking child. Now he felt he had been wrong to do this.

Why had Mrs Sowerby written? Was the boy much worse? Was he dying? In spite of these alarming thoughts, Mr Craven remained calm. For the first time for many years, he felt courage and hope.

And when he arrived at Misselthwaite Manor, the servants immediately noticed he looked better. He went into the library and sent for Mrs Medlock.

"How is Colin, Mrs Medlock?" he asked her.

"Well, sir, he's … different," she said. "He goes outside now. Miss Mary and Dickon Sowerby push his chair into the garden and he stays there all day."

MR CRAVEN COMES HOME

Mr Craven looked surprised. "Where is he now?"

"In the garden, sir. He's always in the garden, although nobody is allowed to go near him."

"In the garden!" said Mr Craven. And after he had sent Mrs Medlock away, he repeated the words. "In the garden!"

He went out of the house, through the courtyard and across the lawn. The flowerbeds were full of brilliant autumn flowers but he did not see them. He crossed the lawn, as if in a dream, and walked along the paths and beside the long ivy-covered walls to a place he had long since tried to forget.

He knew where the door was, even with the ivy hanging over it. But where had he buried the key? He stopped and looked about him. And at that moment, he heard the voices – children's voices! And sounds of laughter and excitement.

Suddenly, the door in the wall was thrown open and a boy burst through at full speed. He didn't see the man near the wall and almost ran into his arms. He was a tall, handsome boy glowing with health.

"Who – what?" said Mr Craven.

Colin looked at him. "Father," he said when he'd got his breath back. Then he stood as tall and straight as he could. "I'm Colin. You may not be able to believe it, but it's true. And it was the garden that did it – and Mary and Dickon. Aren't you glad, Father? I'm going to live for ever and ever!"

Mr Craven took his son's arm. He could hardly speak for joy. "Take me into the garden, my boy," he said.

So they led him in.

They led him through the gold and yellowing trees, and between rows of late-flowering roses. Then they sat down under a tree – all except Colin who wanted to stand as he told his father the story of the secret garden's magic.

"Now," Colin said when he had finished the story, "it need not be a secret any more. I'm never going to get into that wheelchair again. I'll walk back to the house with you, Father."

And so he did, to the astonishment and delight of all the servants who were watching. Across the lawn came Mr Craven. And by his side walked Colin – as straight and strong as any boy in all of Yorkshire.